George Eyre

The Lady of Ranza

And other Poems

George Eyre

The Lady of Ranza
And other Poems

ISBN/EAN: 9783744765596

Printed in Europe, USA, Canada, Australia, Japan

Cover: Foto ©Andreas Hilbeck / pixelio.de

More available books at **www.hansebooks.com**

THE

LADY OF RANZA

AND

Other Poems.

BY

GEORGE EYRE.

ALEX. GARDNER, PAISLEY,
AND 12 PATERNOSTER ROW, LONDON.
1884.

CONTENTS.

Poems.

LOVE-LIT.

OPEN thy lattice, my heart's delight !
Loveliness swims on the air to-night !
Deeply the moon like a goblet dips,
The sea is kissing the shore's wet lips,
Whispers the corn of a secret name,
Blushes the rose for her bosom's shame,
Breath of the bean-bloom softly sighs
Like a maiden trembling in love's surprise.

Open thy lattice, my heart's delight !
Blush not to yield me thy lips to-night !
Whisper no fears, withdraw no charms,
But yield thy soul in my circling arms,
While the earth below and the heaven above
Breathe and whisper and dream of love !

MAIDEN !

WHEN upon the smiling sea
   Shines the summer sun again,
Maiden, truly tell to me
   Shall a memory bring thee pain ?
Memory of a quiet time
   Broken by a vain regret—
Memory of a poet's rhyme—
   Of a heart that holds thee yet ?

Silent is the tuneful key ;
   Shines the summer sun in vain ;
Tears are falling fast for thee,
   Showers from heaven of silver rain.
Let them fall ! my cheek is wet.
Would that we had never met !

AFTER.

'TIS a sweet and sun-lit dream
  That floats o'er me again—
I see the sun-gilt gossamers,
  I hear the hive's refrain,

Again I breathe the scented air
  By the blue, unshadowed sea,
As I walk in the great rose garden there
  Like a careless king, with thee.

But the dream is gone, and for love-lit eyes
  That I thought read love in mine,
On the toil of a slave under smoke-dimmed skies
  The sun scarce cares to shine.

Yet there is rest for the weary,
  And hope is the rest of the heart :
O dearest, in hours most dreary,
  My hope's far home thou art !

In the turmoil and the strife
  Of the roaring city street,
Like a breath of purer life
  Comes thy spirit o'er me, Sweet !

O crush not the chrysalis shell
  Of hopes that are scarce expressed,
But let me dream of days unborn
  When their silver wings shall rest !

For happy am I to think,
  When a day's long toil is past,
It has severed another link
  Of a chain that must end at last.

ANTONY.

LULLED by the pleasant plash of oars,
The silver sheen of summer seas,
The golden gleaming sun,
In soft abandonment of ease
He lay at Cleopatra's knees
Who half a world had won.

He watched the swelling silken sail;
And, stretching far on either side
A crescent curve of foam,
He saw, with eye of languid pride,
His galleys sweep the glistening tide
In dread array towards Rome.

Above him hung a canopy
  Of purple silk and prisming sheen
    Of precious stones and pearls,
  And o'er him bent with tender mien
  The dark smooth-skinned Egyptian queen,
    While round-limbed Nubian girls,

The fairest of their far-off land,
  From fans of scented sandalwood
    Sent fragrance through the air.
  Deep in a dreamland haze imbrued,
  By Beauty's smiles and sighings wooed,
    Marc Antony lay there.

For since on silver Cydnus smooth
  He sank enchanted by her side,
    O'ermastered by her smile,
  His heart has owned no other guide
  Than this dark-bosomed, lawless bride
    Of level-flowing Nile.

Ah ! wild and deep, the noblest know
　The potency of such a spell !
　　The world is Woman's still.
　And he who loves a woman well
　With her would rather toil in hell
　　Than climb alone heaven's hill.

The bright oars flashed, the sunlight shone,
　The cymbals beat, a fair wind blew,
　　While he for whom they wrought,
　Voluptuous, drinking love, like dew,
　From eyes whose depths no measure knew,
　　Lay far from care or thought.

A measured chime of changing tune,
　That flutes and silver cymbals beat,
　　Kept cadence to the oars,
　And all the gay and joyous fleet
　Swept, like a dream, the low and sweet
　　Mediterranean shores.

They passed by many a low, green isle
That, cool in sunlit silence, slept,
Calm mirrored in the sea ;
Mayhap 'twere better to have kept
Home there, and loved, and smiled, and wept,
O Antony, for thee !

As the bright sun that day went down
Far o'er his boyhood's home, the West,
In floods of molten gold,
Perchance his spirit sighed for rest
In some lone valley, unopprest
By all the cares untold

That haunt the ruler of a world.
But when beneath the stars that night
The marshalled navy lay,
Sternly he planned the morrow's fight—
Empires were hanging on his might—
He longed for breaking day.

At last it dawned, and Eastern eyes
Saw Roman triremes flashing far
O'er the Ambracian tide.
Antony rose, the Evening Star
Of Egypt's glory, and to war
Turned from his mistress' side.

As, when the earth lies tranquil fair,
Dark clouds o'er Autumn heavens sweep
Before an unfelt wind,
So swept the navies o'er the deep,
Breaking the waters shining sleep
To floods of foam behind.

As roaring thunder rends the air,
And drowns within the caverned rock
A hermit's holy psalm,
The crash of rushing battle broke,
And shattered with a sudden shock
The silent, sunlit calm.

The battle's terrors black and loud,
The plunge and surge of sinking ships
Smote dread on eye and ear :
A pallor stole upon the lips
Ot Cleopatra ; dark eclipse
She feared her lover near.

But he upon the highest deck,
Mighty as Mars, stood in the sun,
The forefront of the fight :
Well might the bravest Roman shun
The dread *mêlée* where such an one
Smote death to left and right.

With not a cloud upon his brow,
While triumph lit his face serene,
He broke their Roman pride,
As stands a rock the tides between,
And backward breaks their billows green
In spray-showers far and wide.

The sun sailed slowly from the East,
  As Antony from Egypt came,
    Till mightiest they stood,
  It in its Zenith, he in fame :
  Alas ! that such a sunrise calm
    Fell to such sunset's blood !

Now, as the clouds that gather depth,
  And rush in blackness on a gale
    To whelm the Autumn sun,
  The Romans rally, oar and sail—
  The wind has risen—now to fail
    Is empire lost—death won.

"See !" cried the Roman admiral,
  "The sun of Antony has passed
    From its meridian height.
  On ! let the moment be his last,
  And from her throne the harlot cast
    Who rules o'er Roman right !"

With measured beat of blazing oars,
　And foaming rush of warlike prows
　　Bore down the great array.
　Darkling, as storms that thunders rouse
　Together roll with rival brows,
　　The navies met midway.

The tide of war had reached its height—
　A moment more the wave had turned,
　　And Rome had vanquished lain,
　When every warrior spirit burned
　To see the golden guerdon spurned,
　　And all the valiance vain.

And lo! as ship that braved the gale,
　When sudden breaks her rudder band,
　　Drifts aimless on the sea
　Stood Antony—his arm, unmanned,
　Dropped to his side—his lip's command
　　Stopped—pale as death grew he.

As birds that fly at eventide
  In flocks along the yellow sky
    Fled Egypt's sixty sails.
Was heard a groan ; but ne'er a cry
Of anger broke from Antony—
    Love to the last prevails.

Faintly, as hears a drowning man
  The dash of waves, he heard the roar
    Of battle round him roll.
Its fearful joy he sought no more ;
A wilder fire than raged before
    Was flaming through his soul.

" Farewell thy cold embrace, pale Power !
  Of thee Man's soul must weary grow ;
    But, blest as Jove above,
A ten times stormier joy I know—
A bliss worth ten such worlds of woe—
Back to my golden Nile I go—
    Back to thine arms, O Love !"

Cast gloomy in his galley's stern,
   The hero from the fight withdrew,
     And then away—away—
   Swift as a swallow skims the blue,
   With white sail-wings aslant, he flew
     Towards the dying Day.

He followed fast her silver sails,
   And ere the oars of Egypt dipped
     Beyond th' Ionian sea,
   The same low wave that lightly lipped
   His prow, was by her trireme ripped
     To fire-tipped furrows.   He

Heaved one deep sigh, as in the West,
   Like his own glory, sank the sun :
     His hero-heart was human.
   Then, breaking from the mood, as one
   Whose long day's toil at last is done,
   He smiled on her—the smile of one
     Who gave a world for Woman.

IN CITY PENT.

No glorious sky and sea,
　　But city walls
　　Where shadow falls
Around encompass me.

No loving one have I,
　　Sister or wife :
　　Bright things of life
Do not around me lie.

My day in toil is spent
　　Above a street
　　Where countless feet
On pleasure pass intent.

And from my window place
Sometimes I see
Look up at me
Some fair, unwearied face.

Fair, happy ones whose lot
Is softly cast
Where care is past
And canker cometh not.

And at the even chime,
When others hie
To bright homes, I
Pass but a lonely time.

Till often, ere I sleep,
Of wild desire
My heart takes fire—
I wish that I could weep.

Yet sometimes with my pen
I sit and dream,
And soft eyes seem
To gaze upon me then.

Nor would I change my lot
In such an hour
Of pensive power
For wealth that dreameth not.

UNDER THE UPAS.

Away with thee! Shadow of darkness!
  Hence! vanish, thou fiend, from my sight!
Think not thou can'st drive me to madness;
  I laugh at thee thus, here, to-night!

Aye, hideous Phantom of terror,
  I tremble no more at thy look.
Begone to thy dungeon of error,
  And leave—leave me here with my book!

A new light has lit up the pages;
  Thy visage my soul shall forget.
I tell thee I pay thee no wages.
  My soul is not thine—no, not yet!

Thy chains that for long years have bound me
  Shall break.   I shall laugh at their strength.
The power of a God shall surround me,
  And I shall defy thee at length !

A spirit of beauty has fluttered
  From heaven and lodged in my heart,
And hopes of a Future unuttered
  Have said that thy power shall depart.

Begone ! tell me not thou can'st blight them—
  That Hope is a dream of the past—
That thou to thy bed shalt invite them,
  And I shall be chained there at last !

That she—oh ! my own, whom I cherish !—
  Shall fade like a flower at thy breath !
That I, when my sweet visions perish,
  Shall wake in thy loathed arms from death !

Back, Fiend ! Touch me not with thy finger !
　My soul is not thine—no, not yet !
Back ! Out of my chamber, nor linger !
　The seal of my fate is not set.

For beauty can spring out of ashes,
　As springeth that flame in the grate.
So up from my spirit there flashes—
　Out ! Devil ! My dream is too late !

IN A WINTER CITY.

O FOR the hum of summer bees!
  Bees in the bells of the sweet wild thyme;
For the upland brown with hardly a breeze,
  For the idle love and the lover's rhyme!

For the sapphire sky and the silver sea,
  And the golden clouds and the glowing sun,
For the tinkling stream and the silent tree,
  For the one fair face to gaze upon!

CHATTERTON'S LAST HOURS.

WHY should I live ?   The world is not my friend.
Who weeps when dies the tongue, its words unsaid,
That would have warmed cold hearts, made bright eyes
      bend
   To pity.   Who shall care, when I am dead,

Whether the world is colder for the loss
   Of one poor poet, though his heart was true,
And warm with fire that might have burned the dross
   Out of some hearts, lit some dead aims anew !

Who cares for higher aims and visions brighter ?
   Let young ideas seek a useful vent !
We live by precepts of an older writer—
   With what our fathers thought we are content,

Each for his selfish ends, merchant and lord,
   Year in year out, toil, or for treasure's gain,
Or the poor prefix of a senseless word;
   The world is poorer by their bread in vain.

Once in a hundred years a prophet rises
   Burning with other zeal—clear eyes, true heart;
And the old shell of crusted lies surprises—
   Chains fall off at his touch, dark stains depart,

And spirits bent and weary with earth's toil
   Arise refreshed as if with heaven's rain.
He sows his heart's blood in a selfish soil,
   And reaps neglect and madness for his pain.

Would he whose soul is but a ledger weep
   If the Power died that spreads the blossoms out
And bids the Summer come? He still might keep
   What he had gathered—still might trade on doubt.

And the pale poet, lent to earth to spread
   Through life the fairer flowers of love and truth,
Uncared for in his attic may lie dead,
   Slain by the vampire, Greed, that feeds on youth.

THE EAGLE FREED.

UPWARD! upward! the iron bars,
  Broken and twisted, fade below.
Upward under the golden stars,
  Up through the soundless heaven I go!

And the cool wind of my old domain,
  Here in the depth of the boundless night,
Sings through my sweeping wings again—
  Bears me again on its liquid might.

With a·deep breath and a heart on fire
  Lonely again and a king I roam,
Heaven's whole realm for my heart's desire,
  Heaven's blue depth for my pinion's home.

Up on the storm-wind's strength I soar—
  Out on the confines of air and space :
Earth chains canker my heart no more—
  Free, with Forever before my face !

Free ! and my wings are not wings that tire ;
  Beat have they oft at the sun's own gate.
Nothing o'ershadows my heart's wild fire—
  Free—I am free from the things I hate !

Roll on, dark world, in the depth below !
  Star-globes of amber around me roll !
Stronger and bolder my broad wings grow ;
  Burst are the bars that confined my soul !

I SLEEP.

I SLEEP, but my heart is waking,
  And walks in a dream with thee :
Warm light in thine eyes is breaking,
  Is shining, my own, on me.

The winter, Beloved ! is ended,
  The dew on the clover is wet,
The tears of the night are expended,
  The day is before us yet.

LOVE'S DRAUGHT.

MANY a lip may have told thee,
   Many a smiler have sworn
That it was heaven to behold thee,
   That thou art fairer than Morn.

So any fool might have spoken.
   Can a man help having eyes?
But 'neath that beauty unbroken
   Lovelier loveliness lies.

He who can see but the casket,
   Matchless and rare though it be,
But for its beauty can ask it:
   He is unworthy of thee.

Flowers may bloom in thy tresses;
  Smooth as their petals thy brow:
Jewels may glow on thy dresses;
  Deeper thine eyes burn now.

Gay in the moments of gladness,
  Witchery subtler has none.
Then to behold thee is madness:
  He who dare gaze is undone.

But from a witchery deeper
  Do I the darkness unroll:
I have awaked—I the sleeper—
  Deep in thine eyes drunk thy soul.

THE LADY OF RANZA.

ON Arran's western shore, where Ranza lake
Meets with the azure of the open sea,
The mountain breasts of dreaming mother World
In barren grandeur raise their purple domes,
And guard the limpid lake that lies between
In sleeping stillness, scarcely broken by
A mountain linn that falls in snowy spray
Adown a precipice, and, murmuring, flows
In rippling wavelets o'er its shallow bed
Of pebbles to the lonely inlet's shore.

Between the hills, dividing lake and sea,
An islet meets the wave. Upon its breast
A castle stands mossy and grey with age,
Whose battlements on every side approach

The narrow beach, and leave small room for path;
But on the sunniest side a narrow strip
Of ground is cultivated, and sweet flowers
That grow there scent the air of all the isle.

Such is the home of one of Earth's fair blooms
Unfolding into glowing womanhood.
Sweet Lerna is the last of all her race—
Chieftains who held the keep from sire to son.
Buoyant in form and fair of face, her hair,
Escaping from its band, flows down in gold
That rivals e'en the sunlight of the morn.
Her love-deep azure eyes are softly stern,
For she is mistress of her castle here,
But these clear eyes can laugh so merrily
That all who hear her voice and see her eyes
Are bound in love to her from that sweet hour.

But all is bustle in the castle hall,
For Lerna sails across the Sound to-day

To her old aunt Aldina, whom before
She has not seen, for, since the maiden's birth,
Her aunt has never crossed because of age,
And Lerna ne'er has crossed the Sound before.

Now forth she steps down from the castle gate,
Her maidens following into the barge,
And slowly glide they o'er the level sea.

While in the shallows, Lerna gazes o'er
The gunwale down upon the crystal depths
And silver sands, with here and there a bed
Of seaweed, like a tropic forest, twined
And intertwined with trailers, growing there
In all the hues of Autumn, and a fish
Or two at leisure o'er the tangled weed,
Suspended in a sapphire atmosphere.

As swiftly sweep and dip the shining oars,
The maidens three lie languid in the shade

In careless grace, and one her fingers trails
Along the cool, clear water at the side.
The merrier two are talking quietly
And laughing low, as maidens oft will laugh
When talking of their lovers heedlessly.

But Lerna sits in reverie, and dreams
Of the two cousins she has seldom seen—
Her aunt Aldina's sons, who until now,
Have sailed their ship on many a far-off sea.
She thinks of Ronald now, a merry boy
With sunny hair in curls about his brow,
Who used to say he loved her, long ago,
When he sat by her, gathering sea-shore shells.
Impulsive boy he was, whose merry thoughts
Seemed ever rippling sunshine o'er his lips.
And fondly dreams she of him yet, as if
He still were but a boy and she a child
Who gathered shells upon the long sea shore.
His brother she remembers too, and his

Dark hair divided o'er a noble brow ;
And sad he ever seemed, yet kind he was ;
Seeming to her like some deep, cool, clear well,
Unruffled by the storms that blow around.

While Lerna dreams, the barge moves smoothly on,
Till Ailsa's rounded craig is southward seen
Dim through the silver shimmer of the heat,
And one tall ship that lies out there becalmed,
Like some white seabird on the ocean's breast.

The watchman on Aldina's turret top
Has seen the barge glide onward o'er the Sound
And given warning of its coming, so
Comes Eron down with Ronald to the shore
And two or three rough sailors after them.
And there they meet fair Lerna, and the two
Do welcome her with courteous grace, and straight
They bring her from the jetty to the path

That winds, a steep incline, towards the Hall ;
Her maidens slower following.

And as
The brothers walk along on either side,
They cannot help but gaze on Lerna's face,
So pure and lovely in its calmness.   And
When Eron sees those liquid eyes look up
At him, it is as if the sunlight touched
His soul within, and overflooding it,
Filled all his being with a wondrous joy
Unknown to him before.   His brother too,
So lively and impetuous of yore,
Walks quietly, drinking in the low sweet tones
That fall from her bright lips in converse with
Dark Eron.

Presently they reach
Aldina's Hall, and round, as they pass on,
The menials make obeisance to the guest,

And after she has gone, they, clustering round,
Talk wond'ringly of all her loveliness.

But Lerna passes with her cousins through
Low stone-arched passages and dim-lit halls
Into an inner chamber, where her aunt
Lies pillowed round with cushions.

　　　　　When the light
Of her clear, grey, old eyes falls on her niece,
She starts, and smiles, and, stretching forth her hands,
She welcomes her in thin and trembling voice.
" My dear lost brother's only child !" she says,
As Lerna fondly kisses her pale cheek.　　　　.

And there the young sit by the aged a while
And talk of olden days ; and Lerna tells
So fondly of the days of gathering shells,
That Ronald wishes such could come again,
That he might lie beside her in the sun　　　.

And tell how he has loved her since that time :
How on the rolling seas, beneath the sun,
Beneath the moon and stars his heart has dreamed
Of one fair image on a distant shore.
But 'tis denied : and soon a maiden comes
To show the guest her room.

The brothers then
Walk forth into a shady wood, and talk
In absent voices of their coming cruise,
Of men and battles, armourings and stores,
And all things save their guest.

* * * * * * *

The groaning board
Steams with the scents of many a savoury dish,
While many a laugh and jest is heard among
The sailors and the menials of the Hall.
And Lerna's maids, the two that laughing talked

Of lovers, titter with the maidens of the Hall
At all the merry talk ; but one, Irene,
Who trailed her fingers in the rippling wave,
Sits silently in dark-eyed pensiveness,
Till, catching Eron's glance full on her face,
The red blood mantles o'er her blue-veined brow,
And, drooping those long lashes consciously,
She veils the strange dream trembling in her eyes.

*   *   *   *   *   *   *

With Ronald, Lerna climbs the steep hillside.
The sun slants downwards from the western sky,
No zephyr stirs the clear, elastic air,
And silence reigns around them as they go
To see the sun set in the western waves.

The murmur of their talk, like waves that lap
The margin of a lonely mountain tarn,
Comes through the calm, fine air.

And Lerna asks

Him of his voyages in distant climes ;

And he delights to tell her, for her eyes

Look up into his own from their blue depths

The while he tells these strange tales of the sea.

And, as she gazes in that sun-browned face,

She marvels at the wondrous love he bears

His elder brother, to forget his own

Fair deeds.   For Eron ever in these tales

Plays hero.

As they reach a steeper part,

Wild, overgrown with green, a stoney road,

More slowly climbing o'er the rougher ground,

Ronald's eyes steal a glance at the sweet hand

Clinging with gentle pressure to his arm.

Sighing the soft sigh of a sudden wish,

Involuntarily he folds it close,

And blushing, she looks up into his face,

And he looks down, and meets her eyes, and then
A sudden light springs to the eyes of each.

The glorious scene at last breaks on their view,
And there they watch the dying of the Day
Amid the purple calm of evening.
Majestic, slow and glorious sinks the sun
Afar beyond the ocean's gleaming flood.
The grandeur of the silent scene is felt,
And stills the murmur of the lonely voice,
Filling the soul with waves of solemn joy.
But slowly sinks the glory in the West,
And darkly still the ocean lies below.
Yet burn the cloudlands golden, till the rays
Are slow withdrawn, and all is left
In deep and sacred-like repose.

Ronald's voice breaks at last upon the stillness.
"Ah, cousin ! were our Heaven Home as fair
As this, my raptured soul would ask no more,

But, Lerna, does it come amiss that now—
That thus I tell thee all were dark as night
Without thee?   In the sea a thousand suns
I've seen sink gloriously, but ne'er like this.
O Lerna! 'tis thy presence—thine alone
Makes all things fair to me !   Thou art my sun,
My moon, my star!   The whole wide world were dark
Without thy love !   Speak ! say thou lovest me !"

Long linger they on that fair mountain brow,
And starlight falls upon their homeward path,
As down the hill they blithely come apace.
Pale Eron, sitting near the firwood's edge,
Sees their dark figures 'gainst the deep-blue sky,
The manly build of Ronald and the form—
Ah ! how his heart bounds as he sees that form !
The slender shape of Lerna.
                                   When he sees
Her face, a sudden shadow falls upon his soul :

But, with the gentle talk of usual themes,
He walks down with them to the torch-lit hall.

*   *   *   *   *   *   *

As Morning rises from the Orient,
Comes Eron, and forth paces on the sward.
Still there he stands, forgetful of the time,
Deep swallowed in his thoughts, when Lerna comes
To breathe the dewy air, and there they meet.

Now Eron wakens from his reverie,
His face aflame with eager passion's fires.
He seizes there her hand, and, as she starts
Like startled fawn, he, gazing in her face,
Pours out the madd'ning torrent of his love—
The pent-up passion of a mighty soul
In an appeal of agonized suspense.
He waits an answer; but all sound has left
Her bloodless lips, and tears are in her eyes.
At last the words come, slow in utterance—

"We may not—cannot—never shall be more
Than brother—sister! Husband—wife, ah! no,
We cannot be!"

Like marble is his face.
All joy has fled from life for him : the rest
Must all be dull and cold.
One last, long gaze
He took, and slowly dropped her hand, and then
Turned mournfully away.

＊　＊　＊　＊　＊　＊　＊

Gun after gun
Pours forth in thunders death and ghastly wounds.
Mad shouts and hoarse wild cries of men are heard
Above the din of battle. Everywhere,
The foremost in the fight is Eron seen.
Where Spanish boarders swarm upon the ship

His sword a meteor flashes : all shrink back
Before that red steel blade and firm-set face.

Thus, all day long the battle rages fierce,
Nor cease the guns from their terrific roar
Till sunset, when the Spanish fire is slacked,
And Eron stays the thunder of his guns.

Slow rolls the smoke up from the scene of death,
And there the gilded ship is sinking seen.
Her captain stands alone upon the poop—
All else lie low amid their ebbing gore—
One hand upon the mast that bears the flag,
The other on his jewel-hilted sword—
A nobleman, the bluest blood of Spain.
Now Eron's voice is heard amid the silence ;—
"Gallant, Sir Captain ! yield ! the day is ours !"
But calm and dignified the answer comes—
" I yield not, Spaniards die but never yield."

His doom approaches fast.   Unmoved he stands,
His helm bright, blazing in the setting sun,
Whose light streams in a golden lane across
The sea, and falls upon the wrecks of ships.
Now lower sinks his vessel in the waves,
And lower still, and deeper ; then she heaves
In three short breaths, like some great beast in pain,
Upward again she heaves, and plunges down
In wild, majestic grandeur : first the bows,
And last the poop, where stands the warrior,   ·
Surge down beneath the sea.

                    Upon the waves
That pitch and eddy where the ship went down,
Each earnest face long gazes, for a sign
Of that high, noble figure, helmed and plumed :
But far down in the blue depths of the sea
His hand still clasps the mast that bears the flag,
And 'neath the Spanish banner still he sails.

＊　　＊　　＊　　＊　　＊　　＊　　＊

Moaning out of the West the winds arise,
A mighty storm dark gathers o'er the sea,
And drives the ship before its foaming waves.

Far o'er the waters' boundless, tumbling waste,
Between a leaden sky and leaden sea
They wildly fly, scarce knowing whitherward,
While day and night succeed in anxious toil.
When, in a grey dawn, 'twixt the night and day,
The deep, hoarse roar of waves that break their strength
On some wild coast, is heard above the storm ;
And with a crash that rends her stem to stern,
The fated vessel rushes on the rocks.

Wave after wave beats on the groaning ship :
Again the crash comes, and, from where he stands,
A great wave carries Eron overboard,
And washes him up on its crest of foam
Into a little, quiet, sandy bay.

His eyes turn seaward.   Lo ! the ship is gone :
Great beams and wreckage toss upon the waves,
And o'er the storm rises the last, wild cry
Of some brave sailor sinking to his grave.

But, as he gazes o'er the towering waves,
He sees a black speck 'mid the driving surf.
Now lost to sight, now borne in on the foam,
His brother's form is hurled upon the shore :
And, as the wave sweeps back its living waif,
Down rushes Eron, grasps the yellow hair,
And raising Ronald in his powerful arms,
Bears him up from the foaming, angry sea.

He lays him on a bank of soft brown sand,
And chafes his chilly limbs, until the blood
Flows once more through the empty arteries,
And Ronald opens wearily his eyes.

Now as the morning breaks the coast is seen—
Dark beetling crags above a stoney shore,
Where broken fragments of the rock above
Lie heaped and scattered in the churning surf.
But out to sea they gaze in mute surprise,
For there the rounded Craig of Ailsa lies.

In truth, on Arran's shore have they been cast,
And Ronald's heart beats fast with rising hope.
They scale the cliffs that hem the narrow bay,
And higher still ascend, until they find
A cottar's hovel thatched upon the waste.
There, entering, they tell their tale of wreck,
And, as they stand beside the peat fire's glow,
They ask, in earnest tones, of Ranza keep—
If all is well, and peace around the walls.
The goodwife, hearing they are thither bound,
With many a piteous prayer urging them
To gather Lerna's vassals, and defend
The fair young mistress of the island hold

(For she was nurse to Lerna when a babe),
Informs them of a raid, planned secretly,
To carry off the maid by force of arms,
And wed her to a chieftain of the isle ;
For Lerna's lover is upon the sea,
And she waits for him long and faithfully.

The brothers stand revealed before the dame,
And tears start from her eyes in sudden joy
As, running to a corner, brings she forth
Two broadswords for their use, then, eagerly
She sends them off, with her stout fisher son
To guide their steps and lend his lusty aid.

Along the coast they march, fast gathering men
Till, when the darkness hides the hills from sight,
They number thirty, stalwart, brave and true,
Enough to garrison the castle walls.
As night falls o'er the pathway and the sea,

D

They halt, a little space from Ranza loch,
And enter a low hut upon the heath.

When all are slumb'ring round the glowing peat,
Steals Ronald out into the still night air.
His eager heart yearns in him for a sight
Even of the grey walls that surround his love,
So he sets out alone for Ranza's shore.
But, as he walks away into the night,
Another, rising, leaves the peat fire too.
'Tis Eron.

"That I ne'er had loved!" he thinks.
"And yet who could behold those sweet blue eyes—
That tender mouth, and still be proof to Love!
And ah! I would have toiled from dawn to dawn
Rather than she should lose one little joy!"
And, as he sighs, the strong chords of his heart
Yearn passionately for a glimpse of her—

To clasp her but once in one long embrace—
Press one kiss tenderly on her clear brow—
Gaze once more in her eyes, and say "Farewell!"
Alas! it cannot be.

He follows on
Until they climb a hill, and see, beneath,
The castle lying, silent, gray and calm.
No ripple stirs the moonlit lake's expanse :
The scene is peaceful as the heaven above.

Down Ronald bounds towards the beach.
But, as
The bees rise round th' intruder in their hive,
A hundred foemen spring from 'mong the fern
And, with a savage yell, rush in on him.
His broadsword flashes out and bears them back.
With swift, sharp strokes he holds a charmèd ring,
And downward presses toward the open shore.

But numbers gather round—the foe is strong—
Despair unnerves his arm—his guard is down,
When, with a loud, strong shout, a giant form
Bounds from a crag amid th' astounded foe.

Awestruck and paralyzed they stand, until
Three comrades fall beneath that sweeping sword.
Then, like the dogs around the noble stag,
They rush on him ; but round the good blade wheels,
And down the hill he clears an avenue,
Until he reaches Ronald. Then the two
Together fight, nor waste a breath on words
Until they reach the glassy inlet's shore.
Now Eron's voice strikes on his brother's ear—
" Haste ! only one can live—plunge thou and swim,
While I hold back these cowards from thy path !
Think—think of Lerna, Ronald, and her fate !
The Future's bright before thee brother—plunge ! "

But Ronald's soul forbids him thus to leave

His brother, till he sees in Eron's face
Th' unflinching look, and thinks of Lerna's fate.
Then with the words—" Fight! I will bring thee aid!"
He gazes once upon that firm, pale face,
And, plunging in, swims for the moonlit isle.

Now down upon the shore the foemen press
Where Eron stands alone to guard the way,
But as some mighty oak withstands the storm,
He holds them back for long, until he knows
His brother far beyond the reach of harm,
Then, rushing up the hill again, he meets
The chieftain—him who thus would win a bride.
Their broadswords clash together and the blows
Rain fast and hard on Eron.   Suddenly
The plaided chief sinks wounded on the heath—
A crimson torrent stains his tartan's hue.

And now the silent ring that closed around
Springs upon Eron, wearied with the fray.

What can one arm among so many foes ?
He turns his eyes once more upon the isle.
The moonlight floods the calm and lovely scene ;
The castle gate is open, and he sees
His brother gain a footing on the shore.
He sees a vision of a fair white form,
With streaming golden hair, fly down the shore
And clasp his brother fondly in her arms.

Then Eron, shouting forth his battle cry
Of " Lerna !" rushes 'mong his foes and deals
One mighty stroke, and falls upon his face
Dead, and without a single mortal wound.

Before the warriors wake from their surprise
The thirty vassals downward rush on them,
And, like the autumn leaves before the wind,
They scatter over all the mountain side,
Pursued by foes relentless as the storm.

Now, as the sounds of combat fast recede,
A boat glides from the castle to the shore
Laden with stalwart highlanders full-armed.
But, e'er the boat's keel grates upon the beach;
A figure springs off from the gunwale's edge,
Where she had lain concealed within the shade,
And, rushing up, perceives, among the rest,
The form of Eron lying.

Kneeling down
Beside that prostrate form, she raises up
His head, and looks once more upon his face.
No tear flows out to ease the breaking heart,
As deep she gazes in those lifeless eyes—
A strange, wild look upon her pallid face.
At length the boatmen raise her from his side.
She rises, gazing wildly round on them,
And throwing up her arms, gives one wild shriek,
And flees away along the dark hillside.
And nevermore Irene was seen by men.

When wonder fell to reason in their minds
The men uplifted Eron from the ground,
And bore him to the boat, and rowed across,
And laid him softly in a chamber dim.
There, in a little, Ronald came alone,
And knelt and wept beside his brother's form.
Then, when his mind grew calmer, he arose
And brought his young bride in to look upon
The face of him who loved them both so well.

SAILING.

SLOWLY, slowly, sailing, sailing,
  Down the river drifted we,
And the wild wind, wailing, wailing,
  Fled away upon our lee.
Overhead a gull was railing;
Willows in the wave were trailing,
As we slowly, sailing, sailing,
  Drifted down toward the sea.

Was this then my day dream's ending?
  Was my summer idyll done?
I'd been earnest; she'd been spending
  Only pastime in the sun.

Siren-sweet her voice was lending

Passion to my passion's rending,

For she, o'er the lilies bending,

    Heedless hummed an idle tune.

Softly o'er us swept the sighing

    Of the West wind sad and lone,

And it brought the gray clouds flying

    Ever Eastward to its moan.

Sighed the willows low replying,

While 'a wild swan, lonely dying,

Sadly sang her death song, hieing

    To the dim remote unknown.

Darker drove the cloud-wrack o'er us :

    Cliffs arose on either hand :

Leaden waters rolled before us,

    Sullen through the wintry land.

Swifter, swifter on they bore us,
Mid the wild and stormy chorus
Of the waves and winds that o'er us
  Whistled to the dreary strand.

From, the rifted cloud the lightning
  Flashed upon the livid tide,
And the thunder's roar was frightening
  The warm bosom by my side,
For her cheek was slowly whitening,
And her hand on mine was tightening :
Mid the storm one ray was brightening :
  Careless I for aught beside.

Wilder wailed the wind and weirder ;
  Faster drove our shallop on ;
Broken was the helm that steered her ;
  Wind and tide were guides alone.

Closer clung my love : I cheered her,
Trembling for the fate that neared her.
And the wind wailed wilder, weirder,
  As our shallop hurried on.

Flashed the lightning, rolled the thunder,
  Down the current wild we flew,
Seabirds shrieked around in wonder,
  Cliffs, rocks, trees shot past our view
In the distance—ah it stunned her !
Roared the rapids loud as thunder.
On we rushed the black clouds under,
  And the wind demoniac grew.

Mid the noise of winds and waters
  Quivering now her voice I heard :—
"I am one of Eve's own daughters !
  I am ruined by a word !"

Tenderly my own hand sought her's.
Even now my spirit totters,
As it sees the seething waters—
　　Hears again the voice it heard.

In her eyes the tears were starting—
　　" It was I, love, wrought thee this !
Death, for love so true, imparting !"
　　On her lips I sealed a kiss.
Meant it union ? meant it parting ?
One fire through our souls was darting—
Wildly was our shallop starting
　　Down the torrent's dark abyss.

Gone was all the careless spirit,
　　Grave and tender was her face.
Woman's love lies hid, but stir it,
　　Warm and true it shows its place.

Dark the thought, yet we could bear it—
Death was near us—we should share it—
Wild my heart beat, I could hear it
   As we ran that fearful race.

Down the rapids white with fury
   Shot our shallop madly free ;
Round a beetling promontory
   Swift as swallow darted we :
From a cloud dark, lowering, hoary,
Burst a crash of livid glory—
One was left to tell the story—
   One was lonely on the sea.

CONTRABAND.

By a Vagrant Bee.

I SAW fair palaces of pearl
  Within a coral gate ;
I heard a silver-throated merle
  Sing sweetly to her mate ;

There came a zephyr, soft as air
  From gardens of the South ;
I saw, I heard, I lost me there—
  I kissed that coral mouth.

TILL THE SUN WENT DOWN.

THE sunlight slept and the millstream ran,
  And the miller's daughter was fair to see.
"O nought care I for boy or man !
  O happy am I and fancy free !"
And the face beside her to cloud began,
  For a light and careless air sang she.

The sunlight slept and the millstream ran,
  And the miller's daughter was fair to see.
And still she sang "Nor boy nor man
  E'er has been pain of a thought to me !"
And his face beside her was vexed and wan,
  And he bade goodbye. "Goodbye !" laughed she.

The sun was down and the millwheel stopped;
 Still the miller's daughter was fair to see.
Of a sudden the paper before her dropped,
 And a sharp and terrible cry gave she.
Her heart's wild beat like the millwheel stopped:
 "He is dead—they have killed him! and he
 loved me!"

NIGHT.

WHEN the sun smiles on the earth
　　The earth like a bride smiles too ;
When his light dies in the night
　　She weeps for him tears of dew :
　　But when in the morn again
To his love rises the Day,
　　All bright with a glad delight
She forgets night and is gay.

When the shades darken to death,
　　And life like the sun has set,
Let not night, Soul, thee affright !
　　New light shall awake thee yet,
For the eyes wake to a sun more fair
When the death dews have refreshed the air.

J. G.

We do not weep for that a man is dead—
  Men are too many in this world of ours—
  But for the promised thought, the pregnant powers
Death-mown like blossoms, levelled with that head.

Few hearts are fit to lead the van of life ;
  Most can but follow, and mayhap 'tis well,
  And we can ill afford to say "There fell
A promised leader for to-morrow's strife."

Yet surely here there fell as strong a heart,
  At sudden call grew still as true a tongue,
  As beat for right and from the rostrum rung.
Adieu ! The gods have loved thee, and we part.

ACROSS THE HILLS.

St. Valentine's Day, 1882.

THOUGH, thus so far divided,
  My lips caress not thine,
My soul is at thy casement
  To be thy Valentine.

Ah ! leave it not to perish
  Out in the dreary snow,
But in thy bosom cherish
  The thing that loves thee so !

And may the breath that kisses
  These love-red lips of thine
Bear soft the fragrant blisses
  Until they fall on mine !

Deny me not the pleasure !
  Should petals bloom in vain ?
I steal from thee no treasure
  I would not—give again.

Then cast me, Sweet, caresses
  Upon the light-winged air !
I envy that it presses
  The flowers that flourish there.

But many a moor and mountain
  Lies, Love, between us twain,
And at that nectar fountain
  To taste I long in vain.

Yet though, so far divided,
  My lips caress not thine,
My thought is at thy casement, Love,
  To be thy Valentine.

THE BREAKFAST BELL.

" TEN minutes yet !" and he closed the door
 And straightway strolled to the lawn outside.
"Ten years ago I was twenty-four,
 And I asked her here to be mine, my bride.

" My heart had flown to my lips just then,
 I had told her all that I had to tell ;
Her hand in mine, I had asked her—when
 Suddenly clamoured the breakfast bell.

" Ten years of life in an Indian city
 Seem to have left me a young man still.
She is a widow now, wilful and witty—
 Heavens ! she's coming out. Should I—I will !"

" Up with the sun, Mr. Rupee !" "She's charming !
    Up'! yes, to gaze on the roses out here,
Wond'ring if you—" " Mr. Rupee, tea-farming—"
    " Hasn't at all changed my taste yet, I fear."

" O ! so you still admire roses ?"   " Why, yes !
    How can I help it since, ten years ago,
Though you forget it, a rose from your dress
    Dropped on the grass here. I've kept it, you know."

"What ! kept a rose ?"   " Aye, a memory too !"
    " Why, I'd have thought they would both die
        together !"
"Not when the memory kept was of—" " True—
    Now I remember, 'twas sunshiney weather."

" Sunshiney was it ?   I thought it was wet.
    That is, I know the barometer fell—
Fell, and it hasn't recovered that yet."
    " Well it may rise now, Jack. Hark there's the bell."

YOU'LL REMEMBER.

You thought I was shallow as others
  Whose vows light as grasshoppers play ;
You smiled on me but for a moment,
  Then changed—in a womanly way.

Once only you seemed to be earnest—
  I saw the truth dawn on your face.
Ah! that was a moment of rapture.
  Alas for the time and the place !

Had I but been free to have spoken
  What burned on my utterance then,
I know from thy lips would have broken
  The trembling and tender " Amen ! "

But past is that moment for ever—
Its memory never can fade—
I knew that our hearts beat together,
Though little between us was said.

Then in came the Babel of voices ;
They said it was time to be gone :
I turned, sickly smiling, to meet them ;
Your face, as I saw it, was wan.

If down in the shadowy future
Our paths be not destined to meet,
You'll remember, perhaps, will you, darling ?
How one heart once lay at your feet.

THE OLD LOVE'S LOVE.

LIKE alabaster, her face was pale,
  And sadness methought was about her brow.
Ah! none but I could unfold the tale
  Of the pallor and sadness that haunt her now!

Her eyes met mine, and a faint flush spread
  Beneath her skin, like wine in a glass;
She faintly smiled as she bent her head,
  And I stood a moment to let her pass.

Ah! though she has crossed the Rubicon's stream,
  And turned her gaze on the Gorgon's head,
My soul sighs over its byegone dream,
  And I love her still for the love that is dead.

BEFORE AND AFTER.

A WORD, a touch, a glance, a smile,
　A vision of beauty, a dream of bliss,
A wild suspense, a maddening while,
　A low response and a rapturous kiss.

A darkening room, a flickering fire,
　A motionless muser, a deep drawn sigh,
A lonely heart, a lost desire
　And an aching remembrance of bliss gone by.

PASSION-FLOWER.

A Tale of these Times.

I.

Noon is asleep in the village ; the men are away in the
 meadows
Cutting the first of the hay, for the summer was early
 this season.
High overhead in the heavens the sun blazes fierce in his
 whiteness.
Under the shade of deep eaves lie the cottages cool 'mid
 their gardens.
Open the lattices hang, and the brier and ivy around
 them
Toy with the pot-flowers inside, the sweet mignonette
 and the fuschia.

Out on the road not a figure—yes, one in the heat is
approaching.
Dusty and weary he seems, with a knapsack slung over
his shoulder.
Close to the hedge is he walking, where hardly a hand-
breadth of shadow
Shelters a dry withered edging of grasses and thick
growing wild flowers.

Seen but of one is the way-farer : close by the roadside
a garden,
Shaded by green apple trees, with hedges of sweet honey-
suckle,
Faces the white dusty highway.   There by the wicket a
maiden
Pensively lingers a moment.
                              Behind her, away in the sunlight,
Hidden well-nigh by the rose-bushes, dazzling the eye by
its whiteness,

Snowy expanses of linen are waiting the hand of their
    mistress.

But for a moment she lingers.   The stranger approaches
    the wicket,
And courteously asks for a drink, from the vessel of
    water beside her.
Wait! she will fetch him a cup : and she trips up the
    path to the cottage,
While, with a smile on his face, half frolic and half
    admiration,
Gazes he after her, wondering who is the rustic-born
    beauty.

" Here is the cup !"
            " Many thanks !   Like a fresh draught of
    life is this water,
Cool from the hand of a Hebe !"

Standing together a moment,
Such are the words they exchange, and he raises his cap
and has vanished
With just a light thought in his head of a face and a
sweet cottage bonnet.
But o'er the hedge of the garden she watches him enter
the village,
Turning at last with a sigh to her cares in the meadow
again.

When, after sun-down, the shadows came over the roofs
of the village,
Wearily saying her head ached, she quitted the dim-
lighted parlour
When, over farming and politics, sat with her father,
John Ashton.
And as she left them her heart felt a pang of remorse for
a moment ;
Well did she know why he came there—it was not to
talk with her father,

But she was weary and sad, and her spirit was full as for
    weeping.

II.

Down through the lanes, where the moonlight serves
    only to deepen the shadow—

Down 'twixt the high-arching hedges, with velvety grass
    for a carpet,

Where on the night air the scents of clover and meadow-
    sweet mingle,

Loiter the footsteps of two—a youth, tall and noble in
    bearing,

But with a smile on his lip better judged by a woman of
    fashion—

Soft as a dove by his side, a maiden with eyes all
    admiring,

Listening rapt to his words, and forgetting all else in
    his presence.

Not for the first time their meeting since when at the
wicket he tarried.

Often alone has she met him—he stays at the inn in the
village :

Eagerly, secretly, oft has she stolen away to be with him.

Bred in the sunlight the maiden, and trustful and sunny,
her spirit

Drank of the glittering cup of homage the wanderer
offered,

While, like a beautiful flower, a new joy was opening
within her,

Till all her happiness was to be near, to see and to hear
him.

Back has she started, and stands with the tears shining
wet on her lashes,

Gazing reproachfully at him and trembling with fear and
with sorrow.

" Was it for this then, alas ! that I thought to have loved
and been happy ?"

"Marian! dost thou not love me?"

> And tenderly, sadly he says it,

Passing his arm round her form, and gazing down into
her eye-depths.

How can she bear thus to slight him? His heart has
been hurt by her doubting.

But for a moment she wavers, and then, in a wild burst
of weeping,

Bends like a rain-laden lily. His words have prevailed:
she has yielded.

Closer he draws her and presses a kiss on her white,
arching forehead,

Pure is that forehead and stainless. His lips, are they
pure—they are burning.

III.

Silent and dark is the scene. A chamber once noble
and stately.

Many such are to be found in the lonelier streets of a city.

Faded and dim is its grandeur, and where, in the past,
 silks and satins
Rustled and kissed, and the sunshine of smiles lit the
 faces of beauty,
Loneliness reigns. It is winter, and high in the spacious
 apartment
Mist wreaths are floating. The fire, nearly out, on the
 broad hearth is dying.
Hiding her face in her hands, as she bends o'er the
 ashen red embers,
Silently weeps there a woman. The carved cherub faces
 above her
Smile from the other days down on her.

 There, in the corner, exhausted,
Breathing his last, lies a man, and the quivering nostrils,
 and hectic
Bloom on his cheek, and the thin, wasted hand straying
 out on the cover,

Speak of the terrible fire that is burning the life out
within him.

Over his dew-beaded forehead the hair waves luxuriant
backward :

Closed are the blue-veined lids of the eyes that were
wont so to sparkle :

Glorious even in death's grasp he lies, like a wreck in a
sunset.

Motionless have they remained, as hour after hour came
and left them,

Silent, excepting a sob, now and then, from the slight
bending figure.

Winter's short daylight is fading, and over the roofs of
the city

Drearily rises the fog, and the gloom in the chamber is
deepened.

" Marian ! "

Hark ! 'twas his voice, and she starts from her
weeping, and quickly

Moves to his side, with a flush overspreading her grief-
stricken features.

He has awakened at last, and the feverish visions have
left him.

Clear as a spring are his thoughts, and he feels that the
end is approaching.

Faint is his voice as he speaks ;

"Oh Marian! canst thou forgive me?

Grievous and all unrepaired is the wrong I have done
thee—oh Marian !

Gentle and sweet hast thou been, not a murmur of bitter-
ness uttered,—

Speak to me ! Say thou forgivest me !"

"Heaven forgive us !" she murmurs.

Frantic with weeping she buries her face on the pillow
beside him,

Shaking the bed with her sobs.

With unspeakable grief on his countenance,

Taking her hand between his, as something most precious
and sacred,

Speaks he to her in a voice that is trembling with tears.

"My beloved !

Though to the cold, shallow world our love is as something unholy,

Think not all hope gone for ever.   Sweet was the sin,
but ah, Heaven !

Have we not suffered its punishment ?   Marian, may we
not meet yet

Where sorrow entereth not, and our sins are forgiven ?"

Pressing fondly

One lover's kiss on her hand, falls he heavily back on the
pillow.

Wildly she starts, and he smiles, and his lips utter tenderly " Marian !"

Slowly the light fades away from his eyes and the lingering
hectic

Bloom dies away from his cheek.   Alone beats her heart
in the silence,

IV.

Twilight has deepened to night. Not a sound in the
chamber of darkness
Tells of the motionless figure that sits alone still by the
bedside,
Gazing in tearless despair at the face frozen white on the
pillow.

Suddenly over her brow shoots a spasm of pain. She is
thinking
Far, far away, of her home, with its clambering ivy and
roses.
All its old memories stream on her soul, like the sun
through a crevice.
Fair as a dream it arises,—the pure happy home of her
girlhood,—
Sweetly the breath of the meadows came up in the bright
summer mornings;

Softly the chime of the bells floated down on the still air
of evening.

Why art thou tearless, oh dreamer? These joys have
departed for ever.

Slowly, unbidden, arises a grave tender face in the vision

White in its voiceless despair and with tremulous lips, as
it was when,

Late at the wicket that night, she laughed at his offer and
left him.

Strange is the heart of a woman. A sudden paroxysm of
weeping

Bends all her nature before it, till, seized with a terrible
calmness,

Stooping, she presses a kiss full of tenderest love on the
forehead

Frozen in death by her side, then rising, she takes from
his finger

One bright gold ring with her hair in it,—it was the last
thing he cherished.

Putting it on, with the words in a passionate low voice
    delivered,—
" Farewell, my love ! we will meet,—I will meet thee my
    own love in—Heaven !"
Passes she out in the darkness, the gloom of the slumber-
    ing city.

v.

Up from the dark rolling river, under the flare of the gas
    lamps
Slowly a cortege was moving. Till death will the bearers
    remember
How, with a face livid pale, strode a man to their midst—
    bending forward,
Pressed on the dead lips a kiss ; wildly gazed on the
    beautiful features,
Eagerly caught up the hand,—there was no marriage ring
    on the finger,—

Uttered a terrible curse, and rushed from their sight in
the darkness.

Rough men were they and accustomed to scenes such as
this, but their faces

Spoke of compassion mute voiced,—their burden had
nigh been a mother.

VI.

Years upon years have rolled on since that night with its
gloom and its sorrow.

Far from the streets of the city, away from their squalor
and traffic

Full in the broad summer sunshine and deep in its
meadows and cornlands,

Emblem of plenty and peace, lies a farm, from the sounds
of the village

Distant perhaps half a mile.   It is said that its owner has
prospered

More than the most of his neighbours, yet, though on the
    tongues of the gossips
Often with one or another his name has been coupled,
    the maidens
Wait all in vain for his choice.

SHADOW.

WILD as a harp that Æolian rings
  Had I desired to have sung to thee,
But a spirit of sadness has breathed on the strings,
  And the voices of music are mournful to me.

Sweetly the lark in the heavens can sing,
  Rapt in the blue of the quivering air,
But his melody ceases when down on the wing,
  To the earth he descends, fear and sadness lurk
    there.

Brightly the stream in its mountainous home
  Sparkles rejoicing through bracken and glen,
But its gladness is gone, with its sparkle and foam,
  When it winds through the plain 'mid the
    dwellings of men.

Glad thus my spirit when high to the stars

    Hope bears it up through the clouds that unroll,

But it droops, like a bird, when it beats on the bars

    Of the world, and a shadow sweeps over my soul.